I0520330

Our First Swinger Cruise

Andrew and Andrea are celebrating their one year anniversary. They've decided to do something crazy! Follow Andrew and his wife as they decide to experience their first-ever swinger cruise. Every day is a crazy new experience.

Stevie Greenfield

Copyright 2022

Published in the USA by StevieGreenfield.com

First Edition

All rights reserved.

No part of this book may be reproduced in any form
without the written permission by the author.

ISBN#978-1-7371986-2-8

This book is a work of fiction. Names, characters, places
and incidents are the product of the authors
imagination and are used fictitiously. Any resemblance
to actual persons, living or dead is entirely coincidental.

Visit me online at www.StevieGreenfield.com or
www.etsy.com/shop/StevieEroticArt

I thank everyone who helped me with their advice, opinions and editing skills. This is my second book and is based on both a fun sexy cruise and my vivid imagination! I hope you enjoy it!

Introduction

The Beginning

As Andrew and his girlfriend close in on their one-year anniversary, they decide they want to celebrate in a totally crazy way. They talked about flying to Las Vegas and staying at a fancy casino. Or maybe they would spend a long weekend in New City, booking a luxury hotel in Manhattan. Or what about a romantic getaway to Paris?......Nope. All of those options would be fun, but not crazy enough.

After dinner one evening, while sitting on the couch, Andrea leans into Andrew's ear and whispers "Let's go on a sex cruise"

Andrew is shocked. "What? You must be kidding. No way!"

Andrea quickly responds, "we said something crazy.... right? I'm not saying we have sex with strangers. I've been doing some research. They have these swinger cruises where clothing is optional. They have orgy rooms where couples go to have sex with others or just themselves.... or just to watch. They stop at private islands where everyone spends the day on the beach naked. I think it sounds hella fun."

Andrew looks deep into Andrea's eyes. She is sooo cute and sexy. "Show me what you've been looking at. It might be fun to be openly naked.... maybe have sex where others can watch us. But no way am I sharing you!"

"I agree! I'm not sharing you either!"

Andrew looked over the information and it did sound fun...and crazy. It appeared that the cruise was not all about swingers. Many nudists and regular vanilla couples enjoyed the clothing optional freedom, especially the secluded beaches.

So, it was agreed. They would go on a sex cruise! It would be fun and a little crazy!

Day 1   A poolside surprise.

The ship is huge. We have a wonderful room with an outside balcony. There are 1500 couples! There're nudists, here to enjoy being naked. There are the swingers, hoping to meet other couples for sex. The new word for swinging is "being in the lifestyle". And then there are the couples like us.... Lookie Lou's. We're here to experience being openly naked and to people watch....actually its couple watching. I must admit, it's exciting walking around, looking at all the couples and wondering...."are they in the lifestyle?"

On the main floor of the ship is the promenade. This is where everyone walks, checking everyone else out. Many of the couples are dressed to impress. They seem to enjoy strutting their stuff for everyone to admire. It's the best place to people watch anywhere! Andrea and I walk from one end to the other. Back and forth. It's totally cool to stare. There're many couples who notice how drop-dead gorgeous Andrea is. I'm feeling very proud that she's all mine. Quite a few approach us to say hi. It's easy to know who the swingers are. I mean, it's easy to know who's in "the lifestyle." It's the second question they all ask us!

"Where are you two from?" Then, "How long have you been in the lifestyle?"

Of course, as soon as we say we're not in the lifestyle, they politely move on to their next prospects. It's still fun and we're flattered to be so popular. I'm sure it's mostly Andrea they're drooling over. And I have to say, we did meet a few fun couples who are not in the lifestyle!

We spend most of our first day by the pool…. naked! This is a first for us, and it's fun. We watch dozens of couples of every age and shape walk by. We're not experts by any means, but it seems pretty clear to us who are nudists and who are in the lifestyle. Those in the Lifestyle are the "beautiful people" …. tan, in shape and scoping everyone out. Of course, that's just our guess. We don't really know, but it's fun guessing.

Andrew says to Andrea, "let's take a walk around the pool."

Andrea's surprised, "are you kidding? Naked?"

"Why not? No one cares we're naked. And you look fucking hot!"

Andrea looks around. She takes a deep breath, then turns toward me with her sexy smile. "Ok! Let's do it."

We get up. I say to Andrea, "I'll follow you." I want to watch her perfect ass as she walks....and I want to see everyone who's checking her out.

As we make our way around the pool, I feel like everyone is checking us out. Several couples say hi or wave as we walk by. Everyone's so friendly. We approach a group of three couples standing by the pool. They're all tan and in shape. My guess is they're in their early forties. And you know what I'm thinking.... they must be in the lifestyle! Andrea must be thinking the same thing. She turns back towards me with a frightened look on her face. "You go first!"

I take the lead. As we get closer, a beautiful tall, tan blonde says to us, "Welcome aboard newbies!" She gives me a hug, pressing her breasts against my chest.

She quickly moves past me and hugs Andrea. "Sweetheart, you are absolutely gorgeous. I'm Diana."

Within seconds we're surrounded by all three couples. Everyone hugs and introduces themselves. I watch the women and men take turns hugging Andrea and complimenting her on how beautiful she is.

Diana's husband, Ron says to both of us, "So what do you think? Are you overwhelmed?"

I respond, "No not really. Everyone's so friendly."

Andrea chimes in. "I'm a little nervous. I'm not used to being naked in front of so many people."

Rigo's a good-looking Latin guy. He gently pulls Andrea close and hugs her again. "Andrea don't be nervous. We don't bite, unless you want us to."

Everyone laughs. As he steps away, we all notice he has an erection.

Diana teases him, "Rigo control yourself, you'll scare the newbies away!"

Rigo smiles and covers his erection with his hands. "What can I say? Andrea you are quite beautiful....and I'm a man."

Looking towards me, he says, "No offense?"

I respond, "No worries, she's beautiful." I point to my manhood. Watching Rigo hug Andrea then get an erection, made my cock hard as well!

Everyone laughs. Rigo's partner Maddie steps forward. "My turn." She puts her arms around me, pressing her body into mine. Her hands slide down my back. Both hands pause on the cheeks of my ass. She steps away sliding her hand across the shaft of my cock. She smiles and winks. I'm speechless. My cock is now fully erect. I'm feeling awkward and a little embarrassed.

Diana steps forward. "Andrew don't be embarrassed, you have a beautiful cock." Looking at Andrea she says, "Andrea, sweetheart. Would you mind if I touched it?"

Now its Andrea's turn to be speechless. She looks at Andrew, then at Diana. She gives a weak affirmative nod, slightly shrugging her shoulders.

All three women surround Andrew and take turns touching his hard cock. Its fucking amazing. My cock throbs with pleasure. I'm lost in the experience. I look over to confirm that Andrea is still okay with all this attention my hard cock is enjoying. Much to my surprise, all the men have surrounded Andrea! Not only are they caressing her perfect breasts & ass, but she's holding Rigo's cock!

What do I do? I don't want to cause a scene. But this was never going to be part of our crazy experience. Fortunately, Ron comes to our rescue.

"Okay, let's let our newbie friends be on their way."

Diana weighs in, "Yes, yes. Ladies, thank Andrew for the treat and let the love birds take a breath."

Everyone is laughing as they move away from us. I'm sure we have proven to everyone that we are indeed newbies. I grab Andrea's hand. She rushes towards me. She has that crazed turned on look that I have seen many times, but never in a group setting! We say our good-byes and walk away. Several couples who had been watching from their lounge chairs applaud. "Bravo."

Once we get back to our lounge chairs, Andrea says, "Holy fuck!"

I ask, "are you okay?" You're not upset, are you?"

Andrea lays back in her chair and takes a few deep breathes. Her eyes are closed. I patiently wait for her to gather her thoughts. Personally, having three attractive naked women touching my hard cock was fucking hot. But watching the naked men fondling Andrea's breasts & ass....and seeing her stroking one of their cocks was not so hot.

Andrea opens her eyes. She turns toward me and speaks. "Andrew, do you remember when we were out on the lake in Tahoe? I said I was worried that you were turning me into a nympho."

"Yes, I definitely remember, but you were kidding."

"Andrew be honest. What did you think about what just happened? All those women stroking your cock.....and those men touching me?"

Andrea still has that crazed look in her eyes. I think for a moment, then speak.   "I don't know, it was all so unexpected. It was crazy. Everyone naked. All of them so nice and into us. They're all very attractive."

Andrea interrupts, "I know! They all hugged me and pressed their bodies into me. They kissed me and told me how beautiful I was. My mind was spinning."

"And then you said it was okay for them to stroke my cock! I was shocked. What were you thinking?"

"Andrew, I didn't know what to say. And then, all the men surrounded me and started caressing my body. I felt a rush of emotions. It turned me on....that scared me."

"Then you started stroking Rigo's cock!"

"No, I was holding it, not stroking it. But, I know, I'm sorry. I don't know how that happened. Are you upset?"

"No, I'm not upset. It's our first crazy moment. But let's not get any crazier than that.....okay?"

We both laugh and agree. For the rest of the afternoon, we quietly relaxed in the sun and watched all the naked couples walk by.

Later in the afternoon we walked back to our room, cleaned up, and took a long nap.

In the evening we dined at a group table with three other couples. Dinner was excellent and fortunately for us there weren't any lifestylers at our table. Two of the couples were older nudists and the other couple were Lookie Lous like us. After dinner we strolled the promenade and danced at one of the clubs. Surprisingly, once we were back at our cabin, we went to bed, kissed and fell sound asleep. No sex and we're on a sex cruise!

Day 2 Fun in the Sun.

The next morning Andrew woke up first. He glances out of towards the balcony at the beautiful blue sky and turquoise sea. He looks at Andrea, so beautiful, lying in bed. He gently pulls their sheets down, exposing her breasts. He leans in and sucks on her nipples. Andrea opens her eyes and smiles. "Good morning".

I pull the sheets down further. I move down, spreading her legs apart. I run my tongue across her pussy. She moans with pleasure. I look up towards her and whisper, "I'm Rigo."

"Andrew! You're so naughty! No you're not!"

I slip my pillow under Andrea's ass. I slowly slide my hard cock into her drenched pussy. She lets out a moan of pleasure.

Andrea has that crazed look. "Are you still Rigo?"

She's caught me by surprise. "Yes, I can be Rigo. Does that turn you on?" I increase my pace, fucking her harder.

Andrea doesn't say anything, but no doubt we both were turned on. I pound my sweet angel hard. My cock throbs in lust. I explode in ecstasy.

Afterwards we lay in bed cuddling. We don't mention our Rigo fantasy.

We shower, dress and go to breakfast. During breakfast we review today's ship itinerary. Looking at Andrea I ask, "Do you see all these classes? Some sound pretty crazy. Look at this one, "Bondage for beginners, a discussion on light pain stimuli and restraints". And this one, "Bi-curious meet & greet. Meet other bi-curious couples and share your fantasies."

Andrea smiles. "This cruise is looking even more crazy than I imagined. I think we should go to a few classes, then go back to the pool." I agree.

We decide to go to a nudist meet & greet. It's nice. There are about ten couples, in all shapes, sizes and ages. Everyone introduces themselves. Most are seasoned nudists who share their favorite resorts. Like I said, it was nice...but boring! We're both happy when the hour was up.

As we excite the room and head towards the elevator, Andrea reminds me, "Okay remember, you picked that one!"

"I'm bad. I guess crazy is more fun than naked. You pick the next class."

Andrea looks over the activities sheet. "I think I'm going to attend the Bi-Curious women meet & greet. It's for women only."

I'm surprised. "You're kidding...right?"

Andrea is quick to reply, "No I'm serious. You know we've had a few steamy sessions with my BFF, Nicky. We kissed, touched....and sucked your cock! I want to see who attends. I'm just curious, don't worry."

"I'm not worried. I guess if you're curious, that qualifies as bi-curious. What am I supposed to do?"

Andrea gives me that devilish smile, "Well maybe there's a guys only bi-curious class?"

"No fucking way! I'll find us two lounge chairs by the pool. Come and find me after your class."

We kissed and Andrea heads off to her class.

While I'm searching for two open lounge chairs, I see our new lifestyle friends standing by the pool chatting. Before I can look away, they see me. Ron waves me over. Shit! I have no choice but to walk over and say hi.

Ron greets me, "Hey Andrew, good to see you. Where's your beautiful wife?"

We shake hands. Rigo and Jack come over and give me bro hugs…. naked. It feels strange, but wtf. Before I can say anything Diana & Maddie hug me, pressing their beautiful breasts against my chest. "Andrew where's Andrea?"

"Well……she's at a women's only bi-curious class."

Maddie laughs, "That is so sweet. I can answer all her questions. Has she played with a woman before?"

Of course, all eyes are on me. "Not really, at least I don't think so."

Before I can say anymore, Diane says, "Don't worry, it's only day two." All the ladies laugh.

Maddie introduces me to the third couple. "Andrew, I don't think you've met Jack and his wife Lisa." Of course, we hug……that's what lifestylers do. Another bro hug and Lisa, a sexy petite Asian woman, pressing her tits against me.

Ron says, "Hand me your towels. You can have those two chairs. We saved them just in case." Fuck. What can I say? "Thanks Ron, that's great."

No doubt it will be interesting to see the look on Andrea's face when she sees were sitting with the swingers! Yikes!

The time flies by quickly. Ron, Rigo and Jack are all fun guys, into working out and enjoying the naked landscape. I didn't notice Andrea arrive until I heard the ladies greet her.

"Hi Andrea!" Followed by hugs and kisses. "How was your class?"

Andrea definitely looks surprised. She stares at me while being surrounded and hugged by the ladies, with that wtf look?

Andrea responds, "Hi, oh the class was very fun. I was just curious. I'm not really bi."

Maddie quickly responds, "Oh Andrea don't worry. Curious is healthy. We women are the lucky ones. We can be with whomever we want!"

All the ladies laugh and agree. Diana speaks. "Go give Andrew a kiss, then come back and sit with us, we want to hear all about your class."

Andrea comes over, looking fabulous. She leans over and kisses me, and whispers, "What the fuck! We're sitting with them?"

Before I can reply, all the men have gotten up and moved in for their opportunity to hug my beautiful naked sweetheart. It's all hugs and kisses. Everyone loves my baby.

Andrea walks back to our lounge. Diane greets her, "come sit down, we'll put lotion on your back."

Lisa adds, "unless you prefer the guys putting your lotion on."

Immediately all the men turn to hear Andrea's answer…. including me!

Andrea quickly replies, "No, no, I prefer the ladies."

Madeline laughs, "good choice."

All the ladies help Andrea with her sunscreen lotion….and not just on her back. They have her stand while they make sure every part of Andrea's firm beautiful body is protected. Andrea stands with her eyes closed.

All of us watch with envy. I glance over towards the guys, we all were touching our hard cocks. Three beautiful naked women applying lotion to Andrea's hard body is mesmerizing. When my sweet angel opens her eyes, I recognize that crazed turned on look. Holy shit…. where's all of this going?

The next few hours pass quickly. We actually have a fun time. The guys sit with the guys and the ladies stay together laughing with non-stop chat. We all move to the pool to cool off where we reunite with the ladies.

The conversation is all the usual stuff.

"How long have you two been together?"

"Where do you live?"

"What do you do?"

 And our question to them……" How long has everyone been in the lifestyle?"

It turns out that Ron & Diana, have been in the lifestyle for 5 years. They met Jack and Lisa on a local website. They all got together for dinner and immediately felt a connection. The four of them went on vacation together to a lifestyle resort in Mexico. When they were there, they met Rigo and Maddie. The three couples played together all week.

That was three years ago. Since then, they have all traveled together exploring different lifestyle resorts. This is their second time on this cruise.

Diana claps her hands to get everyone's attention. "I'm glad we're all having a fabulous time. Andrew and Andrea welcome to our fun group."

Andrea squeezes my hand and looks at me with a *what's next look*.

Diana notices Andrea's scared look. "Don't worry, you're our non-swinger friends."

Maddie interjects. "It's only Day 2!"

Everyone laughs. Diana continues, "Okay ladies we've had enough sun. We have our spa appointment, let's dry off and go. Andrea's going to join us."

Looking at me, Diana says, "You don't mind, do you? You can hang out with the boys."

I'm completely caught off guard. I look at Andrea, only to see both Lisa and Maddie pulling her away. Lisa looks back at me and winks. "Don't worry, we'll take really good care of her."

As they excite the pool, Andrea is finally able to turn and look at me. She shrugs her shoulders and blows me a kiss. The four of them dry each other and scurry off towards the Spa.

Rigo puts his hand on my shoulder, "No worries, she did say she was bi-curious."

I immediately look up at Rigo. Ron and Jack break out laughing. "He's kidding!"

Rigo doesn't hesitate, "Or not."

Again, the laughter breaks out. I'm the new guy...in the barrel. Typical guy banter. I need to go with the flow. I also need a come-back.

"I can't lie. That would be a hot foursome."

Everyone agrees. "You got that right!"

The Spa

The ship's Spa is amazing. Crisp white walls with ribbons of blue turquoise. Tall expansive ceilings with Michelangelo type murals. Roman columns and beautiful marble floors. The staff has been hand-picked. They're all attractive, slender or fit ladies dressed in tight shorts and sheer tops. Every staff member has a name tag with their country of origin.

A beautiful dark woman greets the ladies. She's tall and slender. Her dark nipples press through her sheer top. She's wearing deep red lipstick that contrasts her beautiful chocolate skin. "Welcome to Spa Erotica. My name is Zala." Her name tag reveals she's from Ethiopia.

Diana's clearly the alpha female of the ladies group. "We have a private room reserved. I think we'd like to shower first."

The ladies follow Zala to a changing room, where they exchange their bathing suits and sandals for sheer silky robes. They're led to a private shower room. Andrea is awe struck. There's a stunning wall of glass looking out to the turquoise sea. A small stream meanders through the beautiful mosaic floor. A light soothing rain falls from the ceiling. The ladies disrobe and enter.

Diana looks over towards Andrea. "Do you like?"

Andrea is amazed. Never in her life has she experienced something so beautiful....so luxurious. "Oh, I love it! Thank you for inviting me!"

The ladies gather and begin washing. They encircle Andrea, while enjoying caressing one another with an intoxicating silky foam. With a small washcloth and their bare hands, they gently soap, then rinse each other. Diana turns closer to Andrea. She's a beautiful tall California blonde with radiant blue eyes. She takes Andrea's hand and helps her gently washes over her breasts. Diana has medium large natural breasts. Andrea is mesmerized. This is all so new. Diana's breasts are so soft, yet firm. Diana moves behind Andrea, sliding her hands around Andrea's waist to her flat stomach. She moves upwards and gently caresses both of her breasts. Andrea can feel Diana's nipples touching her back.

Her mind is spinning, *this is so crazy.*

Maddie turns to face Andrea. She's a gorgeous Latina with black medium length hair. Her hazel green eyes glisten in the rain. She's about the same height as Andrea with perfect enhanced breasts. They look spectacular, perfect in every way. Maddie appreciates Andrea's gaze. She pulls her close hugging her. Pressing her wet firm breasts against her, she whispers, "I'm so glad you joined us." Quickly she turns and backs up towards Andrea until she feels Andrea's breasts touch her back. Andrea places both of her hands on Maddie's small waist then moves to her stomach. Andrea thinks to herself, *I can't believe I'm doing this.* She moves both of hers hands up, soaping Maddie's wet firm breasts. They're so silky smooth but so firm. *They don't feel real.* Maddie moves away as Lisa rotates in. Lisa is an adorable petite sexy Asian kitten. She stands five feet tall at the most. She has a lean gymnast figure. She has small breasts with delicate nipples. Lisa gives Andrea an air kiss and then a hug. She slides her wet silky body around to Andrea's side. Andrea feels Lisa's hands slide along her ass and down between her legs, gently washing her inner thighs. The sensation makes her wet with anticipation. For the most part no one speaks. They enjoy their sensual experience of touch in silence.

Diana finally says, "Okay ladies, I think we're ready. Let's move to the next room."

As the ladies exited the room, no one notices Andrea's crazed turned-on look. Andrew would have recognized it in a millisecond.

After the ladies dry off, they're escorted to a smaller dimly lit room. There're two massage tables. A subtle aroma of incense permeates the air. The walls have a continuous mural that flows from wall to wall. Silhouettes of women in erotic positions, Kama Sutra style. There's a narrow tall table with two lit candles with assorted lotions against one wall.

Diana surveys the room, then speaks. "Well ladies, most of us have enjoyed this room before. Today, Andrea is our guest."

Looking at Andrea, Diana asks, "Andrea, what do you want to experience? Do you prefer to receive a wonderful sensual massage or give one?"

All eyes are on Andrea. She looks at Diana, then everyone else. She's obviously a little nervous. "I'm not sure I know how to give a sensual massage."

Maddie walks over to the nearest massage table and taps it with her hand. "No worries sweetheart, hop up and we'll show you."

Diana takes Andrea's hands, pulling her towards the table. Lisa slips behind her and gently nudges her forward.

Andrea doesn't resist. She feels aroused. Her nipples are hard. She's wet with anticipation. Yes indeed, she's definitely bi-curious.

As she climbs onto the table, Maddie directs her to lay on her back. She looks over at the other ladies and winks. Lisa raises her eyebrows and smiles. Diana immediately places her hands on Andrea's temples and gently begins massaging.

Lisa brings over a vial of massage oil. She pours some into her hands, then passes it to Maddie. Lisa positions herself on one side of the table with Maddie across from her. Simultaneously they extend Andrea's arms and began massaging. They work their way down to her hands. Next, they both massage her feet and slowly work up her ankles, to her calves and then her thighs. Diana moves to Andrea's shoulders, then massages her sides before gently caressing her beautiful breasts. Andrea's eyes remain closed. Her breathing increases. All three of them gently slide Andrea towards the end of the table. As Diana continues caressing her breasts, she gently takes one of Andrea's nipples into her mouth. Maddie and Lisa gently push Andrea's legs apart, bending her knees and placing her feet onto the end of the table. Maddie massages the back of her thighs, then slides her hands to her inner thighs. Her hands ever so gently come within microns of Andrea's glistening pussy. Lisa looks over at Maddie. She smiles and with her eyes, points to the glisten of Andrea's pussy. Maddie smiles and quietly inhales her sexually aroused scent. Diana now begins kissing Andrea's neck and then her mouth. It's a passionate kiss with both of their tongues intertwined. It's at this moment that Lisa runs her tongue across and then into Andrea's pussy. Andrea gasps and lets out a moan of pleasure. Lisa continues to feverishly plunge her tongue into Andrea's drenched pussy. Maddie slips her finger in, carefully moving in and out. Andrea is completely lost in sexual desire. Waves of orgasmic bliss pour through her body. Her breathing increases. Diana stops kissing her. She takes Andrea's nipples into her fingers, squeezing & twisting them. Lisa's tongue is now on a mission to make Andrea cum. Maddie is now fucking Andrea with two fingers.

Andrea moans loudly, "fuck....fuck...oh...oh...ahhh!!" She cums hard. Harder than she has ever experienced in her life! After a short moment, she slowly opens her eyes. She gazes at the ladies who are now holding both of her hands and proudly smiling. "Oh my. That was so incredible. Thank you so much. I've never experienced anything like that…. ever."

Maddie breaks the ice. "I guess you're not bi-curious anymore."

Every giggles, including Andrea. They help her up. Andrea asks, "What about everyone else? We're not leaving, are we?

Diana assures her, "don't worry about us. We enjoyed pleasing you. And trust me, our husbands will be very happy to see that we're all horned up and need to be fucked."

Andrew decided to go back to their room. Its only Day two and they both need to not overdo it in the sun. Nothing will ruin their vacation more than a painful sunburn. Andrews standing out on the balcony when he hears Andrea enter the room. He immediately recognizes that crazed look on her face. "Hey baby, how did it go?"

Andrea flops onto the bed. She closes her eyes for a moment, then looks over towards Andrew. "I'm not bi-curious anymore. I'm a lesbian."

Andrew of course is surprised. "What? What happened?"

"Oh Andrew, I hope you're not going to be upset with me. I had an amazing time with the girls. They're so beautiful, and so nice. We kissed and touched. They made me cum. That's like having sex, isn't it? Are you mad?"

"No, no I'm not mad. And I have to say, I'm not surprised. It's pretty obvious they're all bi-sexual and you were virgin candy. This is a sex cruise. Do you feel like telling me what happened?"

Andrea sits up. "Are you sure you want to hear all the details?"

There's no hesitation in Andrew's response. "Yes, I want to hear all about it. I'm sure it was amazing."

For the next hour or so, Andrea tells him all about her amazing experience. She tells him not only what happened, but all the emotions that ran through her mind. Andrea finishes her story with, "It was the most powerful orgasm in my life."

Yikes! The most powerful orgasm in her life? I have to say, I have mixed feelings about that. I'm happy for her experience. I would love to trade places with her. I can imagine, three beautiful women caressing me and then sucking my cock! Hopefully Andrea will still love being with me. No doubt, it's only day two and this sex cruise is living up to its name.

We both take a nap. We enjoy another group dinner with three new couples. One couple is older, both are doctors and new to the Lifestyle. They explain to everyone that when they have oral sex with others, she places plastic wrap over her vagina! We almost broke out laughing, but they were serious! No thank you!

After dinner, we walk the promenade, dance for an hour, then go back to our room. We snuggle for a while before my sweet angel falls asleep. I guess the most powerful orgasm in her life…. wore her out.

Day 3 The Prominade

We sleep in, cuddle and enjoy our morning love making. This time I choose not to be Rigo. Afterwards, we have breakfast and wander in and out of the shops. We decide to attend a speed-dating class. In one of the big ballrooms there are about forty chairs placed in sets of two about eight feet apart, forming a big square. In front of the chairs there are another forty chairs in sets of two facing them. When we enter the room, we notice almost all of the chairs are already occupied with couples. The instructor waves us over, "hurry find a place to sit, we're almost full!"

We quickly find two chairs and sit down. Within minutes every chair is full. There are about a dozen couples who arrive too late. The instructor apologizes. "For those couples who arrived too late, I'm sorry. But we're going to do it again this afternoon at three o'clock. Come early!"

The next hour is really fun. Two couples face each other. Everyone has three minutes to introduce themselves and ask a few questions, then we move to the next couple. Of course, most of the questions are similar. Is this your first cruise? Is it your first sex cruise? Are you in the lifestyle?

We must have talked with twenty couples. Most of them are in the lifestyle. Everyone else are nudists.... except for one sweet couple who thought they were on a regular vanilla cruise! They were shocked at first. But now they're having a great time. We didn't have time to ask them too many questions, but for sure we said we'd look for them on the Prominade.

Next, we attend a bondage demonstration. We watch a girl tied between two poles. She has both arms and legs spread apart. She's blindfolded, facing us and naked. The instructor demonstrates various flogging techniques with whips, belts, and other strange looking devices. He flicks at her breasts. He takes a riding crop and slaps her pussy multiple times. He spanks her ass until its pink. The woman moans with delight. Then he invites the audience to come up and experience flogging her. It's crazy. Quite a few men and women come on stage to give it a try. Most are pretty gentle. But there's a few who seem to enjoy inflicting pain. In the end, the woman is red with welts. We meet up with her after class. She tells us she totally loved the experience.

Andrea asks, "but won't you be sore tomorrow?"

She replies, "yes. It will hurt to walk, sit and even sleep. But the pain will remind me of my wonderful session."

Andrea and I look at each other with the same look, *are you fucking kidding me!* As we leave the room, Andrea says to me, "no fucking way!"

We enjoy a quiet lunch outside a small bistro. It overlooks a beautiful glass enclosed garden. Afterwards, we go to the gym for a light workout. Our plan is to have a day to ourselves, away from our new lifestyle friends. We need a non-crazy day.

We take our afternoon nap, shower and go to dinner alone......table for two.

After dinner, we find an outside table on the Prominade. We order drinks and enjoy the non-stop parade of couples strutting their stuff.

"Andrew, look at that couple!"

I scan the dozens of couples walking by. And then, there they are! A tall slender woman with black long hair and pale white skin is approaching. She's wearing a short red skirt, showing off her long, beautiful legs. She has matching high heels that sparkle. A snug black bustier hug her slender upper torso. Around her neck she wears a black collar attached to a slender leash. Her master walks behind her. She's also striking with beautiful wavy reddish blonde hair, piercing green eyes and bright red lipstick. She's not nearly as tall, but much more voluptuous. She's wearing skintight leopard leggings with gold spiked heels, that show off her athletic legs and ass. Her black bustier overflows in cleavage. No doubt everyone pauses to take notice.

Andrea is impressed. "Wow! Look at them. They're so fucking hot!"

I laugh. "Is this your new lesbian side talking? The tall one reminds me of Elvira or Morticia."

Andrea responds, "Look around, everyone's watching them."

Soon they disappear into the crowd. We enjoy another round of drinks, then walk over to what is now our favorite nightclub. Fillmore's is a very cool club. Everyone must enter the bar area from the second floor, which overlooks the dance floor. There are small bistro tables and chairs along the railing with a stairway on one side. Below there are more tables and chairs surrounding the dance floor.

While I'm ordering more drinks, Andrea walks over to the railing to check out the action below. With two drinks in my hands, I turn, looking for my sweetheart. Where did she go? I walk over to the railing and look down.

Holy shit! She's talking with that bizarre lady Dom and her collared partner. I immediately head towards the stairway. I quickly descend to the dance floor just in time to see Andrea and the collared woman move onto the dance floor. I look towards the Dom woman. She smiles and waves me over.

She speaks, "please sit."

I place our drinks on the table and sit down. "Hi. I'm Andrew."

For a moment she doesn't respond. She stares at me, then smiles. "Hello Andrew, you can call me Nissa." Looking out towards the dance floor, she says, "and that is my Natasha. I own her."

I detect a Russian accent. "So, you're her Dom."

Nissa looks at me again. Pausing, staring, before she asks, "Yes. How do you know that word, Dom? Is Andrea submissive to you?"

"I wish, but no. Andrea has a mind of her own. I'm not saying Natasha doesn't have her own mind!"

Nissa smiles, "I understand what you mean."

I continue, "I read 50 shades of Grey, I think that's where I first learned about Doms and submissives."

We both watch Andrea and Natasha dance. After a few songs they return to the table. Andrea's all giddy. Natasha is more subdued.

"Andrew this is Natasha. Isn't she beautiful."

Natasha smiles, extending her long slender hand. "Hello Andrew."

I detect another accent.

Andrea turns to Nissa. "Thank you so much for letting me dance with Natasha. I really appreciate it."

Nissa again smiles and pauses a moment before replying. "Andrea you are very welcome. You are so pretty, so……delectable.

For the next few hours, we all dance and have a fun time. The music is too loud to really have a conversation. For the most part the woman all dance together while I try to fit in. Yes, it's kind of weird. But Andrea is having fun hugging, kissing and being flirtatious. Is this the new lesbian side of my sweetheart?

It's around two in the morning, when we all say our good-byes. Nissa and Natasha kiss and hug Andrea. I watch them press their bodies into Andrea and passionately kiss her. They tell her she is beautiful. Andrea does not resist.

It's a pleasant surprise when Nissa turns towards me. She hugs, then kisses me on both cheeks. "Andrew, you are a prince. Thank you for sharing your sweetheart with us."

Next, Natasha hugs me, then kisses me.....on my lips. She looks deep into my eyes and smiles. She kisses me again, this time slipping her tongue into my mouth.

"Thank you." She whispers.

Andrea and I stagger to our room. We have had a little too much to drink. Once again, we have managed to have another crazy experience.

Day 4   SPF?

This morning we wake up a little hung over. There isn't any lovemaking. We shower, dress and head down to the promenade for coffee! We find a quiet spot to sit, I have a few questions for my sweet little baby.

"So….we've met a fun group of lifestyle couples, where you basically were seduced by the ladies. You proclaimed to me you think you're a lesbian. Last night we danced all night with two very attractive ladies, who clearly were way more interested in you than me."

Andrea starts to say something, "Andrew…."

But I have more to say, "no, please let me finish. I'm not upset, but we came on this cruise as a couple. I think its cool that you're enjoying all of this girl-girl attention, but I'm feeling more like an observer."

Andrea looks deep into my eyes. She reaches out and takes my hand. "You're right. Everyone is so sexually open. All these beautiful women touching and kissing me really has caught me by surprise. It's so easy to flirt with them. It's a turn on, and it doesn't feel like cheating. I'm sorry."

"I totally get your attraction to the ladies. I would love to be in your shoes. I'm okay with it. I want to have some crazy fun too. I'm just not sure how to make that happen."

Andrea leans over and kisses me. "From now on, we'll do everything as a couple. I promise."

Andrea gives me a devilish smile and says, "Let's go find our new friends by the pool."

I'm not sure what she's thinking, but I feel my cock getting hard. "Okay."

It's easy finding our new friends. They're very happy to see us.

Diana and Lisa see us first and walk towards us. "Newbies, welcome back! I hope you two are having fun. We all missed you yesterday."

Diana hugs and kisses Andrea. "We're so happy to see you."

She turns and hugs me, pressing her breasts into my chest. She pulls back just far enough to kiss me and have her nipples still touching me. She smiles and looks down at my semi hard cock. Her hand gently grazes along my shaft as she steps aside for Lisa.

Lisa also hugs, then kisses Andrea. "Hi sweetie, you look amazing." She turns towards me. She looks down at my now almost hard cock. I'm not sure if I should feel embarrassed or proud. As Lisa moves in to hug me, my cock touches her stomach and is pushed upwards. It becomes sandwiched between us. It feels amazing. Lisa looks at me and smiles. "Andrew you naughty boy." She gently rubs my now hard cock with her body as she reaches up to kiss me.

As she pulls away, she grabs my hand and pulls me towards our new friends. I look back towards Andrea. She's walking hand in hand with Diana.

Ron and Rigo can't help but notice my raging hard on. "Dude what the fuck."

Maddie comes to my rescue, "Andrews just happy to see us." She rushes over and grabs my cock and leads me to an open lounge chair. "You and Andrea will have to share." She gives me a quick kiss and turns to greet Andrea.

This is all so crazy. We're all naked. Having a hard on is no big deal. Grabbing my cock in front of her husband is also totally ok. Wow…. this is heaven.

Of course, the men swarm around Andrea. They all want their opportunity to press themselves into Andrea's young firm breasts and kiss her. She works her way through the gauntlet of hugs and kisses towards me. I can't tell if she's enjoying the attention or not.

She finally reaches our lounge chair and quickly sits down. We only have a few minutes of privacy to chat before everyone will return. "Andrew, this is so crazy." Andrea looks at my hard cock. "What's with that?"

Now I feel a little embarrassed. "I can't help it. Diana, Lisa and then Maddie all pressing their tits against me."

Andrea giggles, "tell me about it. They did the same thing to me, and then the guys rubbed themselves against me. My nipples are hard and my pussy's wet."

Soon our new friends are all sitting around. The fun sexual banter begins. Maddie gets the ball rolling. "Gentlemen, I think we all need lotion on our backs. Can you help us? You can't choose your wife!"

There's no hesitation from the men. I look at Andrea. "What do we do?" Maddie grabs my arm, hands me her lotion and says, "Don't be shy, it's just lotion on my back." Andrea gives me her *why not* look.

As I move over to Maddie's lounge chair, Rigo takes my place! I squeeze Maddie's lotion into my hands and started with her shoulders and neck. I work down her firm yet soft back. Maddie purrs, "that feels amazing."

I glance over towards my sweetheart. Andrea's eyes are closed. Rigo has worked his way to the small of Andrea's back. I turn away, I don't need to see where his hands are going next.

I decide to play it safe. I move to Maddie's calves, working slowly up to her thighs. Maddie moves her legs apart, exposing her shaved pussy. I feel my cock harden. I slowly begin massaging Maddie's exquisite ass. As I worked in the lotion, I press her ass cheeks apart, exposing more of her glistening shaved pussy. I'm lost in lust. My hand gently brushes across her ass button and down towards her upper thighs. As I grasp her inner thigh, my hand gently nudges up against Maddie's wet pussy. I let one of my fingers ever so slightly penetrate her pussy. Maddie's wetness feels sublime. She gasps in pleasure.

Her moan brings me back to reality. What the fuck am I doing! Holy crap. Did anyone hear Maddie moan? I look up towards Ron and Jack. They're massaging Lisa and Diana's feet. Do I want to look over and see what Rigo is doing with my sweetheart? Is Andrea watching me? I turn to look. Andrea is facing away from me. Rigo is massaging her ass and inner thighs!

Diana saves the day. She sits up and says, "Okay ladies, I think we are thoroughly safe from the sun. Boys, we're all very grateful." The men stand up. The ladies slowly roll over onto their backs and sit up. I look over at my sweetheart. Yup, as I suspect, she has that dazed turned on look. She looks over at me and gives me a sleepy smile.

Jack says, "Is it our turn?"

All eyes turn to the queen...Diana. "Sorry Jack, maybe next time. I think you all need a cool dip in the pool." Everyone laughs. As the men move towards the pool, Maddie reaches out and grasps my arm. "Thank you, Andrew. You have wonderful hands." Then she whispers, "and fingers." She takes her finger and places it in her mouth. I smile, then look around. Did anyone hear that? And I still have a fucking hard on!

I grab my towel. Andrea notices my cock. She laughs. "Andrew!" Of course, everyone looks over. Ron yells over, "Come on horn dog, you for sure need a cool dip." Lisa adds, "Andrew do you need me to put some sunscreen on that beast?"

I'm clearly embarrassed. I look over at Andrea. She still thinks its funny. "You can't blame me." Maddie pipes in. "It's my fault. I think Andrew likes me."

I wrap my towel around me, take a small bow towards Maddie and head to the pool. The ladies applaud, including Andrea.

What was I thinking? I was lost in lust. I can't believe I pressed my finger into Maddie's pussy. Should I tell Andrea? How would I feel if Rigo had done the same thing? My mind is spinning....and my hard cock is now limp. Another crazy day.

I must admit, we are enjoying our new friends. The guys hang out in the pool checking out the different couples, making our "guy" comments. The ladies periodically join us, snuggle up to their partners, then go back to their lounge chairs. I think they prefer being alone more than being with us. All the ladies are so fucking hot...and they know it. The pool servers keep the drinks coming. We order a couple of pizza's for lunch.....and salads for the girls.

By the end of the day, we we're all needing a nap. Ron calls it a day. "I think we've had enough sun. Diana, have you had enough?" The queen nods yes. Ron continues, "how about we all meet up for a late dinner. I'll reserve a table for the 9 o'clock sitting in the main dining room?" Everyone agrees. I look over at Andrea, she nods yes. Okay then, I guess having dinner is fairly safe.

Day 4   Part 2. Nighttime Fun

Andrea and I take our usual nap, get dressed and head for dinner. This will be our first experience having dinner with our new lifestyle friends. We both are somewhat excited and nervous.

Andrea and I sit together. Lisa is to my left with Diana across from me. Ron is sitting across from Andrea, with Rigo, of course, next to her. As we're all sitting down, I look over at Maddie. She gives me a sad face, then blows me a kiss. Lisa sees Maddie's sad face. She playfully sticks her tongue out at her, then kisses my cheek. I look over at her husband, Jack. He gives me a wink. I look across the table to Diana. She smiles. "How does it feel to be adored?"

Andrea squeezes my hand. We look at each other. No words are necessary. Dinner turns out to be really fun. We talk about everything, except the lifestyle. Afterwards we decide to go to our favorite dance club. Everyone dances with everyone. I dance with my sweetheart, then switch and dance with Lisa. Maddie and I catch a slow dance. She presses her hot body against me and kisses my ear. My cock grows hard. I know she can feel it against her body. She purrs, "Andrew, I'm glad you like me."

Andrea dances with all the guys and of course, all the ladies. Women are so lucky. They can kiss and hug anyone they choose. All the ladies are dressed in tight, short sexy dresses. Watching them is a treat.

After several rounds of drinks and lots of dancing, Diana looks at us. "What if we give you a tour of the playroom?"

Andrea and I look at each other…. gulp!

Before we can say anything, she continues. "Don't worry, we're not going to seduce you. The playroom is an amazing place. You have to see it to appreciate it. We'll give you a tour. After, you're free to leave, or you two can play together."

Maddie adds, "or you can stay and watch us."

Ron reassures us. "No pressure. We're going up to the playroom. It's on the 10th floor. Think about it. Talk it over. Whatever you do is fine with us."

Jack adds, "It's all about having fun and new experiences."

Everyone stands up from the table. We all hug and kiss. Diana says to Andrea privately, "come take the tour, then leave. You really should at least see how beautiful the playroom is."

We watch them leave, then sit down. The bands on a break. We have a few moments of quiet. Andrea looks at me. "What do you think?"

I respond, "What do you think?"

Andrea smiles. "You said you wanted to experience some craziness together. Let's take the tour. You can decide if we should leave.... or if you want to fuck me."

Well, that caught me off guard. "Okay. Let's take the tour."

We hurry to the elevator and head to the playroom. The entire tenth floor is the playroom. As we exit the elevator, there is the subtle aroma of lavender. There are huge stands of flowers everywhere. The lighting is dimmed. It's like a giant atrium. Thirty-foot glass walls with a domed ceiling. We follow a stone path to the entrance. There's a small line. Ron sees us and waves us over to join them. Everyone is happy to see us. Of course, there's more hugging and kissing. When we get to the entrance the attendant hands us a basket and lets us pass through to the next room.

I ask, "what do we do with this?"

Jack explains, "Before we can enter the playroom, we have to undress. They will give us towels. Your clothes will be waiting for you at the exit."

My mind is spinning. Let the craziness begin! I look over at Andrea. She and everyone else are already undressing. Why am I stressing? We've all been naked by the pool. It's just a tour…. naked, with friends who are swingers!

We enter the playroom wrapped in our towels. It's incredible. Towering glass walls, palm trees, roman columns and flowers everywhere. There are open showers, a small pool and several large spas. It's exactly how I would imagine the Greek bacchanals. Dim lighting with misters strategically positioned create a romantic vibe. A wide path meanders through a maze of beds of all sizes. Some are positioned so anyone can watch. Others are more secluded.

Most of the beds are occupied. Whatever you can imagine, is happening. Couples, threesomes, foursomes and more, all naked and openly having sex.

We pause to watch a woman on all fours. She's sucking a man's cock, while another guy is fucking her from behind. I glance over at Andrea. She seems to be in a trance.

At another bed there were four women sitting on the edge of the bed blindfolded. Various men were taking turns getting blow jobs.

As we near the end of the tour, there's a path chained off with a "reserved" sign. Diane turns towards us, "I hope you enjoyed the tour. As you can see, everyone on this cruise loves to play. The exit is just around that turn."

Ron points to the sign. "We have a more secluded bed reserved. You're both welcome to check it out. Feel free to watch...or just play together."

Everyone gives us a kiss and hug. Ron unchains the path. We watch them disappear. Looking at Andrea, I ask, "Do you want to check it out?"

Andrea has that crazed turned on look I have seen many times. There's no hesitation. "Yes."

We let ourselves in and continue down the path. When we arrive, there's a huge, canopied bed. Everyone is coupled together with their spouses, cuddling and kissing. We watch Lisa begin sucking Jack's cock. Ron moves down between Diana's legs to pleasure her. Maddie and Rigo are kissing.

They wave us over, pointing to an open spot near them.

I feel Andrea pull me as she walks towards that side of the bed. We climb onto the bed. Andrea lays down on her back next the Maddie and Rigo. She looks amazing. I crawl towards her. She spreads her legs as I position myself on top of her. I kiss her. No doubt, my sweetheart is in her crazy turned on mode. We kiss passionately. I move down and suck on her erect nipples. I move down farther, pushing her legs apart, plunging my tongue into her wet pussy. She moans loudly.

Suddenly, Maddie moves towards Andrea and kisses her. Soon they are in a feverish kiss fest. Rigo moves in behind Maddie. He starts eating her pussy from behind. Maddie moans her approval. Next, Rigo inserts his cock and begins fucking her. I decide to follow his lead. I slip a pillow under Andrea's ass, then press my hard cock into my sweetheart. The Andrea and Maddie stop kissing as they are now caught up in the pleasure of being fucked.

Rigo and I are fucking our wives next to each other! This is fucking hot! I Look at my sweetheart, then I look at Maddie, on all fours, being pounded by Rigo. I glance over towards Diana and Ron. Diana is on all fours, going down on Lisa. But it's Jack not Ron who's fucking her from behind! Lisa is sucking Ron's cock! Holy shit! My cock is rock hard! This is the craziness I was hoping for.

I look back at Maddie. Our eyes connect. She crawls towards me, pulling away from Rigo. She presses her body hard against me, passionately kissing me. She plunges her tongue deep into my mouth. I fall backwards onto the bed. Immediately Maddie is on top of me. Our eye-to-eye contact is like a trance. Maddie is a crazed hot Latina. Black hair, black piercing eyes and full red lips. She has a spectacular sexy body. Smooth beautiful tan skin, perfect enhanced breasts with dark erect nipples. I feel her grab my cock and press it up into her wet pussy. Holy fuck! I don't want to break our stare down, but I need to look over towards Andrea. Maddie moves in close and smothers me with deep passionate kisses as she begins riding my hard cock. We are face to face, inches from each other. Her eyes look deep into mine. She is consumed with lust.

What do I do? I'm consumed in lust. I decide I'm not going to worry about anything. It's too late for that! Maddie's so fucking hot. I roll us over so that I can take control. Maddie spreads her legs. "Fuck me." *Oh yes baby, I'm going to pound the fuck out of you.*

As soon as Maddie pulled away, Rigo did not waste any time. He moves towards Andrea kissing her passionately. His hand slides down her flat stomach towards her wet pussy. He teases her clit and begins to finger her. Andrea knows immediately this is not Andrew. Rigo's kisses and scent are different. She opens her eyes. Fuck! Andrea looks at Rigo. He's strikingly handsome, with black hair and green eyes. He's tan, smooth and muscular. She's too aroused to resist. Rigo moves down, pushes her legs apart and presses his cock into her. Andrea watches. Her mind and body are filled with sexual desire. Watching another man.... a very attractive man, fuck her, intensifies all her emotions. Orgasmic waves poured through her body.

I glance over towards Diana. She's now on her back with Jack fucking her. Lisa has pulled away. She crawls towards Maddie and me. She kisses me, then kisses Maddie. Lisa is beautiful. A petite Asian woman with a super fine gymnast body. Staring at me, she lays back on the bed next to Maddie. She spreads her legs and says, "fuck me, Andrew." I look down at Maddie. She smiles.

"Fuck that little bitch." Maddie moves, so that I can move towards Lisa.

A flash of reality interrupts my Nirvana moment. I'm fucking Maddie and Lisa. Jack is fucking Diana. Where's Rigo......and Ron! Fuck! Do I look? Even if I don't look, my mind's imagination is spinning. I look at Lisa. She looks like a teenager. Fuck it. I go down on Lisa's tight shaved pussy. She moans loudly. I push her legs a part and press my hard cock into her super tight pussy. Holy fuck! I slowly start fucking her, going deeper with each stroke. Lisa is so snug, it feels amazing. She groans loudly, "fuck yes. Fill my pussy with your cock." Maddie has moved behind me. I can feel her breasts pressing against my back. She's kissing my neck. She has her hand on my balls helping press my cock into Lisa's pussy. Lisa looks so young. My hard cock feels huge in her tight wet pussy. I'm mesmerized watching my cock slowly slide out, then slam deep into her pussy. Maddie's hand is still cradling my balls. "Fuck that pussy!" I'm lost in lust, powering fucking Lisa's tight wet pussy. Maddie's pressed against my back, breathing into my ear, holding my balls. My urge to cum is imminent. The buildup is sublime....and then I explode in orgasmic ecstasy.

Rigo has placed another pillow under Andrea's ass. He's holding her spread legs a part, one in each hand, as he fucks her hard. Andrea is lost in lust. Watching this strange man fucking her is an incredible turn-on. Ron moves closer. He kisses her, then sucks on breasts. He looks up at Rigo. Without saying a word, they agree to switch. Ron moves in between Andrea's legs and presses his cock into her. Andrea is in a trance, she watches. Ron is the oldest of the group. He's probably in his mid-forties, taller and more muscular than Rigo and Andrew. He has dark brown hair with a little gray on the sides. He has beautiful blue eyes. Ron's hard cock fills Andrea's pussy. She feels the difference. He feels amazing, stimulating all her erogenous zones. Andrea moans loudly. Ron loves seeing her moan with pleasure. He shifts to his power fucking mode. Rigo moves down to assists with holding Andrea's legs a part. Ron is now free to fuck Andrea with everything he has. Never, ever has Andrea been fucked like this. Her ass and pussy are elevated on several pillows. Her legs are being held spread a part....and Ron's massive cock is slamming into her pussy. She loves it! Out of nowhere, she moans loudly, and everyone hears her, "Fuck me! Fuck me! Yes! Yes!"

This of course catches everyone's attention, including mine. Andrea's howls of sexual pleasure pull me out of my nirvana moment. Instinctively I look towards Andrea. Holy fuck! Ron and Rigo are double teaming my sweetheart! Fuck! The sight is surreal. WTF! What do I do? Andrea's yelling for more. Everyone is watching.

Maddie pulls my face towards her. She looks me in the eyes. "Let her have her moment." She kisses me. I do my best to let it go, but I can't block out the sounds of Ron grunting in ecstasy as he blows his load into my sweetheart!

The fuck frenzy has subsided. My lust and desire have been replaced with many different emotions. Everyone begins to migrate to their spouses. Lisa whispers to me, "Go be with her. Hold her. It was just sex."

I crawl over to my sweetheart and spoon in behind her. The other couples do the same. Slowly each one gets up and quietly leaves until its only Andrea and me lying on the bed. I kiss her back. Well, I did say I wanted for both of us to experience crazy. Was this too crazy? After about ten minutes, we quietly get up, shower and walk hand in hand to the exit. We get dressed and head to our room. Andrea is exhausted and I'm mentally reeling. We kiss good night, I say "I love you." My sweetheart has a sleepy smile. "I love you too."

Day 5 The Aftermath

Andrew woke up later than usual. He reached out to his side to gently touch his sweetheart. Andrea isn't there. He immediately opens his eyes. She isn't in bed. Sitting up, he scans the room. He looks out onto the balcony....and there she sits looking out at the ocean. Andrew quickly throws on his sweats. He quietly sits down next to her.

"Are you okay?" he asks.

In a quiet shy voice, Andrea replies. "I don't know."

"Do you want to talk about it?"

"I don't know."

"Is it about last night?"

"Fuck yes!"

Oh shit.... this could be bad. "Andrea, I'm sorry. Everything went too far."

Andrea turns to face Andrew. "Why are you sorry? It was my idea to go on this cruise. It was me who went to the Spa with the ladies and had girl sex. I'm the one who wanted to tour the playroom....and it was me who wanted to go see their secluded bed."

Andrea becomes more emotional. She continues. "Andrew, I let Rigo fuck me! Then Ron fucked me!"

My mind is spinning. My poor baby is full of regret....and she doesn't know I was fucking both Maddie and Lisa! "Baby, I'm so sorry you're struggling with what happened. It was all too crazy. I'm sorry you're feeling terrible."

Andrea takes both of my hands. "Do you remember when I went to the spa with the ladies? They seduced me and I enjoyed it....no, I loved it. I told you I thought I might be a lesbian."

I laugh. "You're not a lesbian. You discovered you have a bi side. I think that's wonderful."

Andrea gives me a smile. "Andrew, last night we were.... not really making love. We were having sex. I was all turned on. Then I smelled a different scent, and someone kissed me. I knew it wasn't you. When I opened my eyes, it was Rigo. He started playing with my pussy. I didn't know how to react. It was so unexpected. Watching him turned me on more. Then he pushed my legs a part and started fucking me. Andrew he was fucking me!"

"Okay baby, I hear what you're saying. I'm not sure where you're going with this."

Andrea is even more animated and emotional. "Andrew, I was so turned on. Ron came over, kissed me....and I watched him fuck me. They both were fucking me! I was in this crazy turned on trance."

"Calm down baby. I see you're full of emotions. I understand you were in some crazed state of mind. Are you sorry it happened? Are you worried that I might be upset?"

Andrea pauses. She takes a deep breath. She takes a sip from her cup of tea. "Andrew, I think I'm a nympho. The sex was amazing. I liked it....no, I loved how I felt. It was crazy, intense....so insane! Are you upset? Do you still love me?

Holy shit! My mind is spinning. This has totally caught me off guard. It's like a double sword blind side. Andrea liked.... loved, being fucked by two men she hardly knows. But I too was in the same crazy trance. I fucked two very hot women. Are we now swingers?

I look at my sweet baby. She looks nervous. I sense she could cry at any moment. "Baby, I'm not upset. I agree last night was fucking crazy. I have something to tell you. I was in that same crazy trance."

Andreas confused. "What do you mean?"

"I had sex with Maddie....and Lisa."

Andrea looks shocked. "You fucked Maddie and Lisa?" I nod yes.

Andrea breaks out into a laugh. "You fucking nympho! I was so worried you wouldn't understand. I don't ever want to lose you. I love you so much. Do you want to know the best part about last night?"

"What baby?

"After it was all over, you came over and snuggled against my back. I felt safe. I felt your love. I never want to lose that."

We both hug. "I guess we're in the lifestyle. Should we go see our new friends?"

Andrea is now in her happy mood. "Yes, let's go be with our friends. But first I want to hear all about your experience."

"Really? Do you really want to hear those details?" I was squirming a little.

"Yes!"

We showered and went down for breakfast. I shared with Andrea the whole story. How it started with Maddie and how Lisa joined us. I noticed a glimmer of that crazed turned on look in Andrea. I think she really is a nympho. Who would have guessed?

On the way to the pool I say to Andrea, "Let's play a little trick on our friends." I explain my idea as we walk. She agrees.

Down at the pool our friends are all lounging by the pool. Ron asks the group, "so do you think we will ever see the newbies again?"

Diana responds. "Unfortunately, I think not. You and Rigo were pretty intense.

Lisa speaks. "I think Andrea will either love what happened or feel bad about it."

Maddie adds, "I know Andrew enjoyed himself."

Jack laughs. "I think you both enjoyed yourself. You wanted him as much as he wanted you."

Maddie agrees. "True that."

Diana speaks. "I'll miss them both. They were both so sweet."

Everyone agreed. Ron sees us walking towards them. "Here they come….and they're not looking happy."

We walk up and stand looking at everyone. I look serious, Andrea is looking down. "Hey everyone. We have something to say to all of you." All eyes are on us.

"This morning, Andrea and I talked about last night. We talked more over breakfast. Last night was not what we expected. It was way too crazy. With that said……"

Andrea looks up. All eyes shift to her. "Last was fucking crazy……we loved it!"

Everyone cheers! Ron jumps up. "You fuckers! You had us going!" Everyone surrounds us for a group hug.... with kissing, of course. All the ladies hug and kiss Andrea.

Lisa kisses me. "I'm so glad you're part of our love family."

Maddie kisses me, pressing her tongue into my mouth. "We're going to have so much fun together."

Diana hugs me. "Welcome. I hope we can play soon." I smile and respond. "You are the Queen. Your wish is my command."

Diana kisses me, "Good answer."

Jack hugs Andrea, "Welcome. I'm looking forward to knowing you better." Andrea smiles and coos, "Me too."

Rigo hugs and kisses Andrea's neck. "You are beautiful and amazing." Andrea gives him a quick kiss on his lips. "Ditto."

Next Ron turns to Andrea. He looks into her eyes, takes a deep breath and says to her. "Andrea thank you for last night." Andrea is silent for a moment. Everyone has turned their attention to her. "Ron, you were amazing." Andrea hugs Ron, pressing her body into him. "Thank you!"

As Andrea steps back, everyone cannot help but notice Ron's hard cock. I can't resist, "What the fuck Ron! I think you need a dip in the pool!" Everyone laughs. Ron is embarrassed. He grabs his towel to cover himself. "I think you right. Come on boys, let's take a dip." With that, the guys all head for the pool. The ladies hover around Andrea all wanting to know her thoughts about last night. The guys are the opposite, they welcome me aboard, but there's no mention of last night. While the ladies want to hear all the details, the guys were not interested in how much I enjoyed fucking their wives. It's a given.

As the afternoon wanes, Diana and Ron make an announcement. "Today was fun. Tonight, is couples' night. Everyone is on their own. Enjoy dinner together...enjoy the evening together. We can all meet up tomorrow. Everyone hugged, kissed and packed up to leave.

Andrea and I enjoyed a wonderful dinner for two at the Sushi bar. We danced a little afterwards, then went to our room. We watched a movie in bed. Andrea stroked my cock, but we did not have sex.... or make love. This cruise has been amazing. I don't think it can get any crazier. I wonder what it will be like to fuck the Queen, Diana.

Day 6   Nissa's Penthouse

Andrew woke up later than usual. Once again, Andrea was not in bed. He can hear the shower running. He decides to get up and sit out on the balcony and wait. When Andrea comes out of the bathroom, he gets up and walks back into the room. "Andrew, its getting late. If we don't hurry, we'll miss breakfast."

"Okay." Andrew quickly showers and gets dressed. Once they are down at the promenade, they have their usual breakfast. Coffee and a croissant for Andrew, tea and bagel for Andrea. Andrew looks over at his sweetheart. "You know we haven't made love or had sex for a few days. We seem to be caught up in group sex."

Andrea looks up at Andrew and smiles. "You're right. Do you want to go back to our room?"

"No. I'm fine. I'm just mentioning it. We only have one more day. Our lives will go back to normal when we get home. Let's go to the gym like we planned."

After breakfast, we go to the gym to workout. After, we enjoy a healthy protein shake for lunch at the juice bar.

We don't get to the pool until the afternoon. As usual our new lifestyle friends are all relaxing at their usual spot. It's all hugs and kisses when we arrive. The ladies kiss & hug Andrea, then take turns pressing their breasts into me with a kiss. The guys all take advantage of pressing themselves against Andrea's hot slender body.... with a kiss. I relax in the pool with the guys, while the ladies giggle and talk non-stop.

A few hours later, Diana announces to the guys, "Tomorrow is our last day. We're going to the spa one more time." As all the ladies gathered their things, Andrea comes over to me. "I guess we're going to spa."

I smile at her. "Okay little lesbo, have fun."

Andrea looks a little embarrassed. "You don't know for sure anything will happen."

"Right baby, have fun."

Andrea smiles, then sticks her tongue out as she scurries towards the other ladies. We all wave good-bye.

Jack sarcastically says, "I think they love eating pussy as much as we do."

Rigo agrees. "More!"

I interject, "I don't blame them."

When the ladies reach the spa, they change into robes, and enter one of the private shower rooms. After disrobing, they move to the center of the room and begin washing each other. First, they apply a rich luxurious foam over their bodies. Andrea washes Maddie's slender back. This is a new experience. The first time the ladies had taken her to the spa, they seduced her. She had been the passive receiver of their affections. Not this time. The thought of caressing another woman's body arouses her. Andrea reaches around and gently washes and caresses Maddie's beautiful breasts. Maddie purrs. Andrea's head spins with sexual excitement. She boldly slides her hands down Maddie's flat stomach and into between her legs. She gently strokes Maddie's pussy. This is a definite first for Andrea. Her heart's pounding, she's feeling herself becoming lost in that familiar trance of desire. Maddie whispers, "My pussy's wet. Press your fingers deeper." Andrea feels her nipples harden. She doesn't feel nervous at all. Without hesitation she presses her fingers deeper. She feels Maddie's wet slippery love juice. Maddie moans louder. It turns them both on.

Andrea feels Diana press up against her back. She begins by washing her back. Diana then massages Andrea's firm ass. Diana slides her wet hand in between Andrea's ass cheeks, pausing for just a moment to fondle her ass button. Soon Diana's fingers are gently fingering Andrea's pussy. Andrea's head is spinning in desire. Lisa moves in behind Diana. Soon everyone is lost in an orgasmic fingering frenzy. Maddie and Andrea climax first, followed by Diana. Glowing in the aftermath, they put on their robes and leave the room. Diana says to Lisa, "Thank you." Maddie kisses Andrea on her cheek.

They enter the next room. It's the massage room. There are four massage tables and four very athletic women dressed in bikini tops and short shorts waiting. The next hour they all receive wonderful non-sexual massages. Afterwards as they're leaving the spa, Diana tells the ladies, "I'm not going back to the pool. I'm going to my room to lie down." All the ladies agree. Andrea texts Andrew. "Everyone is going to their rooms for a nap. No hurry, enjoy the pool."

When Andrew makes it back to the room, he finds his sweetheart asleep on the bed. He quietly lies down next to her and falls asleep.

Several hours pass before they wake up. They shower and dress. Andrew suggests, "Let's go down to the promenade and have a drink. We haven't people watched since we first arrived." Andrea loves that idea.

Once on the promenade, we find a great outside table at one of the bars. It's fun watching the couples strutting like peacocks. Andrea grabs Andrew's arm, "look, there's Nissa and Natasha!" She stands up and waves. Of course, they wave back and walk to our table.

Nissa hugs Andrea. "Andrea my sweetheart, I cannot believe we are finally seeing you two again. Where have you been?"

Nissa leans over and gives me a quick kiss on both cheeks. Natasha hugs Andrea, then turns to me, kissing me on my mouth. She smiles and winks.

Before we can answer, Nissa continues, "we're going to dinner, please come join us. You must tell us all about your week."

I look at Andrea. She smiles and nods yes. I concur, "Okay."

We all enjoy a wonderful dinner at the exclusive Italian bistro, Como Va. We talk about the classes we attended. We talk about our new friends but decide not to get into too many details. Nissa was born in the Ukraine. She now lives in New York City. Natasha grew up in Germany and now lives with Nissa. They have been a couple for five years. They both are very fascinating. Nissa owns two leather & fetish boutiques. Natasha handles the accounting.

After dinner there's an awkward moment. What now? As we're all getting up from the table, Nissa says, "I have a surprise we want to share with you. Come, follow me."

I look towards Andrea. She shrugs her shoulders as if saying, *why not?*

We leave the restaurant and walk towards the elevators. But Nissa doesn't stop, she continues. As we're walking, I'm following behind. I have a wonderful opportunity to scope each of them out.

Nissa is wearing a tight short black sequined dress. She has a beautiful athletic body. Her legs are amazing. She has well defined calves, toned hamstrings and quads. Her ass looks rock hard. The dress is backless. I admire her slender waist and defined back. Nissa glances back. She smiles. Nissa is quite stunning with her reddish blonde hair and piercing green eyes. The low cut of her dress shows off her beautiful, enhanced breasts.

Of course, my sweetheart is equally stunning. She is about the same height as Nissa, but much more slender. Andrea also has spectacularly gorgeous legs attached to a perfect heart shaped ass. She has a slender waist and back. Andrea has medium natural breasts that in my opinion are perfection.

Natasha…. wow. Tall. She's wearing stiletto heels that make her close to six feet tall. Super slender with long beautiful legs and a hot tight small ass. She has a slender waist and back. When she turns sideways, she looks pencil thin with her flat stomach and small breasts. I love her look. I cannot help but imagine fucking her. Natasha's black hair and red lipstick contrasts her pale white skin. She walks slowly behind Andrea, giving me ample time to study her ass. She knows I'm watching. She glances back ever so often with her beautiful green eyes. Dam, I want to fuck her!

We stop at a private elevator, where there's an attendant posted at the door. Nissa flashes her key pass. He opens the door, and we all enter. Andrea is excited. "Wow! This is so cool. Where are we going?"

Nissa smiles. "It's a surprise sweetheart."

As the elevator ascends, my mind is spinning. Here I am, with three beautiful women! Is this going to be my crazy night? Will I get to fuck all three women? I love that I'm the only cock here. We pass the tenth floor. Finally, the doors open at the top floor. It's the penthouse floor. We enter a beautiful atrium with a glass ceiling. There are only two doors. One is gold, the other one is a deep red. We follow Nissa towards the gold door. She opens the door, steps to the side and says, "After you."

We walk in…. OMG! We enter a large living area with tall ceilings with a glass dome overhead. There's a wall of glass and a large balcony facing the ocean. The floors are white marble with veins of gold. A large faux animal skin is strategically placed in front of two yellow ochre sofas that face a huge flat screen tv. On the opposite wall is an LED lit beautiful wet bar with what looks like an onyx top. We are both awestruck. I cannot even imagine what this must cost.

Andrea looks at Nissa in astonishment. "Nissa this is so fucking amazing!"

Nissa smiles, "I'm glad you approve." Looking towards Natasha she says, "Natasha, show them the balcony." Natasha slides the glass doors open as Andrea and I walk towards her. The view from the 12th floor is spectacular. When we walk back into the salon, Nissa says, "Come. Come, we need to celebrate." She places four glasses on the counter. She then holds up a large square ice cube with her ice tongs. It's about three inches by three inches, and perfectly clear. Natasha drops one into each of the glasses. Next, she adds a sliver of lemon peel. From the bar freezer she pulls out a bottle of Vodka. The bottle says CLIX.

"We in Ukraine love our vodka. This is our finest." She than fills each glass. Holding up her glass, she says let us toast. "Do kokhannya i seksu!" Everyone drinks.

Andrea asks, "What does that mean?"

Nissa responds, "My sweetest, I will tell you later." She blows her a kiss. Natasha sets an oval mirror on the counter. Next, she opens a small ornate box. Using a small gold spoon, she places a small pile of a luminescent white powder onto the mirror. As soon as she begins chopping it with a razor blade, I know exactly what it is......cocaine. I can tell Andrea isn't sure what's happening.

Back in college, my roommate would sell small packets of coke to help with his tuition. It's an amazing drug. I still remember some of those crazy fun parties! As I recall, women in particular love it. It makes them horny as hell!

Natasha lays out four thin lines of the magical powder. She looks up at Nissa.

All eyes are on Nissa. She looks at me, "Andrew, I think you know how wonderful this treat is."

I respond, "Yes, but it's been a while."

Andrea speaks, "What it is?"

Nissa says, "First watch, my innocent sweetheart."

Nissa takes a short gold straw. She places one end into her nostril and snorts in one of the lines. She hands the straw to Natasha, who does the same. They both smile. Natasha hands the straw to Andrew. He looks at Andrea, then snorts in the third line. He hands the straw to Andrea. She's hesitant. Andrew assures her, "You will love it, trust me."

Natasha also assures her. "Andrea, you will feel wonderful."

She places the straw into her nostril and inhales deeply. "Fuck, that feels so weird. What's going to happen now? Is this LSD?"

Everyone laughs. Nissa explains, "no, it's not LSD. It's some of the finest cocaine from Peru. I have a close friend whose family imports Alpaca sweaters to New York."

Andrea is surprised. "Cocaine! What's going to happen next?"

I reassure her. "Don't worry. You are not going to feel anything but wonderful."

Nissa taps on the counter to get our attention. "Everyone I have one more surprise! Follow me."

We set our glasses down and follow Nissa into the next room. It's the master bedroom....and its fabulous. The lights are dim, a sliver of light surrounds the room along the top of the walls. There's a mural on the ceiling. It looks like a Greek orgy, Michelangelo style. There's a wall of glass and a smaller balcony to the right. In the center of the room is a huge bed, accessible from all four sides.

Nissa directs Natasha to show us the smaller balcony as she excuses herself and enters the bathroom. The small balcony has a clear plexi-glass floor! We're on the 12th floor! What a rush! Andrea and I cling to the railing as we look down.

The vodka and cocaine are taking effect. We're both feeling great!

As we enter back into the bedroom, Nissa walks out of her bathroom completely naked! She walks slowly across the room. She stops and turns away from us. We gaze at her beautiful, muscular legs and rock-hard ass. She has chiseled calves. Her hamstrings are amazing. Nissa'a slender waist connects her defined muscular back. She extends her arms, showing off her deltoids, biceps and defined triceps. Wow! She slowly turns to face us. She looks fucking amazing. Six pack abs, muscular quadriceps and perfect large, enhanced breasts. I wouldn't say she looks like a bodybuilder. No, she has the perfect blend of defined muscles and a beautiful woman.

Andrea is speechless...almost. "Holly fuck Nissa! You are fucking stunning." She walks towards her. Nissa pulls her close and kisses her. "Take off your clothes."

Natasha grabs my hand and pulls me along as she moves towards Andrea. She turns Andrea towards her and kisses her while Nissa unzips her dress. Soon my sweetheart is also naked. Everyone is kissing and caressing my sweetheart. I'm going along with the flow, but I'm thinking "Fuck! Is this going to be about Andrea and not me?"

Suddenly Nissa and Natasha turn towards me. Nissa unbuttons my shirt while Natasha unbuckles my pants. Nissa kisses me pressing her large, enhanced breasts into my chest. I feel my pants fall to the floor. I step out. Natasha pulls my briefs down and off. I feel Natasha's mouth engulf my hard cock! I feel Andrea press up against my back and kiss me. Yes!

Nissa pulls Andrea away as she walks over to the edge of the bed. She gathers a few pillows and arranges them so they can comfortably sit and lean back. She snaps her fingers summoning Natasha. I watch Nissa spread her legs, exposing her beautiful, shaved pussy. Andrea is definitely in her turned-on trance. I'm sure the coke has kicked in. Andrea spreads her legs apart as well. Natasha walks towards the bed, pulling me along.

"Andrew come here." Nissa is gently stroking herself. I drop to me knees. The scent of her pussy makes my cock throb. I move in closer. I glance over towards Andrea. She's focused on watching Natasha, who has dropped to her knees and is within an inch of Andrea's pussy. I watch Natasha run her tongue across and into my sweetheart's pussy. Andrea closes her eyes and moans with pleasure. I look up towards Nissa. She's watching me. I turn my attention to my task at hand. I press my tongue into Nissa's pussy.

She moans, then whispers to me, "good boy."

I work my tongue in and out of Nissa's pussy. She moans with pleasure.

I feel her hands grasp my hair and gently pull me up. She moves back onto the bed. She wants to be fucked. I climb onto the bed. I move up between her legs, then press my cock into her wet pussy. Nissa moans as she watches me.

I glance over towards my sweetheart. Natasha has removed her clothes and has moved up in between Andrea's legs. She has silky smooth pale skin. Her upper torso is slender and long, as are her arms.

Andrea lets out a moan, then gasps, "Oh my." She's startled. She opens her eyes.   I look down…. holy fuck! Natasha has a cock! She's a trans!

Everything and everyone freezes to a stop. I look towards Nissa, who's silent, then speaks. "She's still a beautiful woman."

I look to Andrea, who in spite of her surprise, is still in her aroused turned-on state of mind …. enhanced with cocaine.

She looks at me and gives me a sleepy smile. "I'm okay."

And with that comment, Natasha begins again to press her cock in and out of Andrea's pussy. No doubt I'm also high on coke. Watching Natasha fucking my sweetheart is very arousing. She is so beautiful. Earlier, I was hoping to fuck her.

I turn my attention back to Nissa, who has been watching me the entire time. My cock is rock hard. I press it into Nissa and begin fucking her…...harder and harder. I look up towards Nissa's face. She has a devilish smile. "Good boy Andrew. I love your cock."

I'm lost in this most wonderful immersion of lust and desire. The coke has enhanced every sensation. I shift to power fucking Nissa. It feels amazing. I glance over to Andrea. Natasha looks amazing. Her slender sexy torso is fucking my sweetheart…. it's so hot. Andrea is also lost in desire. She moans loudly. Natasha also shifts to power fucking. We have definitely lost our minds.

I feel the need to cum building...growing stronger. Nissa must sense this as well. She pulls away from me. WTF? Suddenly Natasha engulfs my cock with her mouth and takes me deep into her throat. Nissa commands me, "Fuck her mouth, Andrew. She wants to swallow your cum." I'm close to cumming. I'm completely lost in lust. I begin fucking Natasha's mouth harder and harder. The buildup is exquisite. The sight of Natasha, this beautiful creature adds to my desires. I'm holding her head with both hands as I slam my cock deep down her throat. I've lost my mind. I cannot stop. I explode in ecstasy. At the same time, I feel Natasha suck hard, pulling out every drop of my cum. The sensation is beyond anything I have ever felt. I howl in total orgasmic bliss.

Natasha pulls away and lies back onto the bed between Andrea and Nissa. All three women are looking at me. "What?"

Nissa smiles and says, "Well done Andrew. I thank you for allowing all of us to enjoy a new experience."

I look first to Andrea, who blows me an air kiss. Natasha smiles as she licks her lips. Nissa continues to stare. My mind is numb. Never in my wildest fantasies would I ever imagine tonight!

Never! Yet, I have said this same thing to myself, several times this week!

"Nissa, this whole week has been crazy, but tonight was over the top crazy! I don't think Andrea and I will ever forget it. Thank you for an amazing experience. We're both very grateful for your friendship....and Natashas."

What was I supposed to say? It was fucking hot....and fucking crazy! For sure, the coke or whatever we put up our noses allowed us to take this unbelievable sexual journey. I'm curious what Andrea thinks.

We all get dressed, hug, kiss and say our good nights. Andrea and I hold hands as we make our way back to our room. Neither of us speak. We quietly go to bed and drift off to sleep.

Day 7 The Grand Finale

I woke up the next morning staring up at the ceiling. I'm in deep thought about last night. Holy fuck Batman! We were totally out of our minds. What did Nissa have us snort up our noses? Natasha is a trans! She fucked Andrea....and we were both turned on by it. My mind is spinning. I look over at my sweetheart. She's awake, eyes open and quietly thinking.

I turn towards her. "Are you okay?"

"Yes, I think so. Are you?"

I reply, "I was just thinking about how fucking crazy last night was. What did we snort up our noses?"

Andrea sits up and turns to face me. Yikes, she has something to say....and I'm not sure what!

"Andrew, I love you so much! I thought this cruise would be a fun experience. I had no idea that it would open me up sexually to who I really am. This cruise has changed me forever. And all of it happened because you were so open and accepting of everything. You're so amazing." She hugs me.

I'm somewhat stunned. Where's this conversation going? "Baby, I love you too. We said we wanted crazy, and we got it."

Andrea continues, "Andrew it's way more than that. I love my lesbian side. Sex with women is amazing. I love our new lifestyle friends. I want to go with them on their next vacation. Fucking each other was such a turn on. I love Nissa and Natasha. I hope they invite us to New York."

I'm speechless.... almost. "Sweetheart, I think this week has been amazing. It's way more than either of us could have imagined. I like our new friends too. I agree let's keep in touch."

Andrea interrupts. "Andrew, I'm a nympho! I love that part of me. When I get turned on it's like a sexual trance. I get crazy. And because I feel safe and secure with you, I have the freedom to be me. I love you so much. I'm feeling so happy."

Mother fuck! Excuse my French. My sweetheart is telling me she's a happy nympho. She loves sex.....with her girlfriends, with our new lifestyle friends and with our new trans-woman friend! And she's thanking me for letting it all happen. My mind is beyond spinning. But I must be careful. Andrea is always full of emotions. Right now, she's full of happiness. And I must admit I have enjoyed this crazy sexual journey.

I take both of Andrea's hands. "Baby, I love my lesbo nympho. As long as we take this sexual journey together and we're honest and open with each other.... let's both be nymphos."

Andrea squeals, "Yes!"

We kiss. Finally, just the two of us make passionate love. At one point while I'm fucking my sweetheart, I look at her and say, "Am I Riggo or Natasha?"

"Andrew you slut! You're you, the love of my life!"

The sex is amazing.

After a late breakfast, we head to the pool to spend our last day with our lifestyle friends. Although I should probably now refer to them as our new friends, since we too are in the lifestyle. It's hugs and kisses followed by a day in the sun. There's the typical sexual banter. We both feel like we belong. It feels great. We make sure to exchange our numbers with each other. I can sense they're delighted to have us onboard.

Jack makes an announcement. "Tonight's our last night together for a while. I'm going to reserve a table at the Chop House for eight. Are we all good with that?"

I look at Andrea. She nods yes. I wonder if this means one more time in the playroom. Will I have an opportunity to fuck Diana?

Suddenly I receive a phone call. I look at the number, I don't recognize it. I answer it anyway. I immediately recognize the Ukrainian accent, it's Nissa.

"Andrew thank you for picking up."

. "Hi. What's up?"

"Andrew, I'm calling because I want to offer you a very special opportunity. It's our last night onboard. The ship Captain is hosting a very elegant private dinner. Only the penthouse guests are invited. It will be very extravagant. French Champagne, caviar, lobster, the best of everything. He has given me permission to invite you and Andrea. I cannot tell you how lucky you are. You must tell me yes or no now. I'm sorry, but that's how it must be. The captain never allows guests, but he is Ukrainian and a dear friend."

"Yes! Yes! Thank you so much! I can't wait to tell Andrea, she will be so excited. You are so amazing!"

Of course, after I hang up everyone including Andrea is watching me. "Sorry guys, we've just been invited to a private dinner with the captain."

Andrea's the first to respond. "What? The ship's captain just called you?"

"No. No. Evidently, on the last night, the ship captain hosts a private dinner for just the penthouse guests."

Before I can finish, Diana interrupts. "Are you kidding! You're invited to the captain's private dinner! How the fuck did you pull that off?"

Lisa is equally stunned. "We've only heard stories, but it's supposed to be the most lavish dinner ever! Only the rich and famous are invited."

Maddie weighs in. "Andrew what did you have to promise? Does the captain get to fuck your sweetheart?"

Everyone laughs. I try to explain, "We met a wonderful female couple who invited us to dinner, and then to their penthouse.... which was amazing. They just called to invite us to the captain's dinner."

Everyone agrees we're lucky as fuck. For the next hour all they can talk about are the stories they about the infamous captain's dinner. We definitely feel lucky. No doubt this cruise has been a never-ending crazy experience….and according to Andrea, life changing.

We really didn't bring anything fancy to wear. That of course is not an issue for Andrea. No matter what she wears, she looks fabulous. I, on the other hand, did my best with slacks and a shirt.

The penthouse elevator attendant escorts us up to the 12th floor. He quietly waits for Natasha to answer the door before leaving. We're greeted with kisses and hugs. Natasha discreetly slips her tongue into my mouth and winks. She looks amazing, dressed to impress. She's wearing an elegant tight black dress. Its short enough to show off her gorgeous legs. She's also wearing a black collar with diamonds. Her lipstick, nails and shoes are red.

Nissa waves us over to the bar. She hugs me, kissing both my cheeks. I apologize for my boring shirt and slacks. She reassures me, "Do not worry Andrew. You didn't know this would happen."

Nissa turns to Andrea. She looks her up and down. "My sweet candy, you look delicious. She hugs her tightly, then kisses her passionately on her mouth. Andrea is surprised and a little embarrassed. She glances towards me. "Wow.... thank you."

"Come. Come. Let's have our favorite cocktail before we go. She pours us our usual CLIX vodka with one crystal clear rock of ice... with a sliver of lemon.

"Do kokhannya i seksu!" Nissa looks at Andrea and says, "My sweetheart, it means "to love and sex!"

We all agree and drink. Next, Natasha pulls the magical box from under the counter. She places the mirror before us, then opens a small vial of luminous white crystalized powder. As she begins to chop it into a fine powder, Andrea nudges me with her elbow. I look at her. She's all smiles.

Nissa, the ever-observant Dominatrix smiles, "Andrea my sweet candy, do you love how my magic powder makes you feel?"

My sweetheart blush's a little, then smiles and says, "I love it!"

"Do kokhannya i seksu!" Everyone toasts again!

We all snort our line. Nissa says, "We can do this again later. We better be on our way."

We enter the elegant dining room. It's on the top floor. The entire ceiling is a mosaic of clear and colored glass creating the flying horse Pegasus. We're greeted by the staff of officers, then handed a glass of champagne. Next, we meet the captain, a tall good-looking man in his fifties. Silver grey hair, blue eyes and a great smile.

"Welcome." He shakes my hand, then kisses Andrea on both cheeks. "Nissa says you two are her very special friends."

Looking directly into my eyes, he continues. "You are very fortunate."

He shifts his attention to Andrea. His eyes slowly and intentionally scan her beautiful body. He kisses her hand. "Enjoy the evening."

What can I say? Every day of our cruise has been amazing, crazy and more than we could ever imagine. Tonight, is beyond opulent. It's everything Nissa promised and more. Nissa steals Andrea away from me, spending most of the evening strolling arm and arm meeting and chatting with the handful of wealthy guests. Natasha is my arm candy as we do the same. Everyone's so friendly. There are only four penthouse suites. Two of the couples are older. The men are dressed in tuxes, wearing their gold Rolex's. The wives are in gowns, blinging in jewelry. The third couple are two gay gentlemen flamboyantly dressed. One is an older man deeply tanned with a shaved head. He's wearing a white tux with yellow shoes and cummerbund. His younger partner is also deeply tanned. His shoulder length brown hair is tinted with green and pulled back into a ponytail. He's wearing tight plaid silk overalls, no shirt, with a green bow tie! They both appear to be wearing mascara. It may sound crazy, but they look great.

 I watch Nissa and Andrea make their rounds. All of the men enjoy fussing over how beautiful they are......especially the gay couple.

Natasha and I mingle, but I feel so self-conscious in my beige dockers and short-sleeved powder blue shirt! The two older couples are polite towards me and mesmerized with Natasha's beauty. They fawn all over her. As we approach the gay couple, Derek and Joseph, I watch them look me up and down and roll their eyes. Politely they shake my hand, then move past me to gush and coo over Natasha. I wonder....do they know her secret?

At dinner we all sit together.... sort of. Natasha is next to me, on my left. But Andrea and Nissa are sitting across from us. I try to get Andrea's attention without saying anything to see if she thinks this is strange, but no luck. The coke has kicked in and she's on cloud nine. Every time we make eye contact, she smiles and blows me a kiss. She's in her happy state of mind.

The entrees are fabulous, all paired with reserve wines or vintage French champagnes. Caesar salad with the dressing made at the table. An exotic soup. Fabulous fresh French bread. An incredible Steak Diane prepared at the table with lobster! Cherries Jubilee also prepared right at our table. Then our choice of a Cask 33 forty-year tawny port or an amazing XO Cognac. Wow! Double Wow!

All through dinner the coke is working its magic. Andrea and I feel amazing. We're so happy, immersed in this once in a lifetime experience. We haven't a care in the world....and we're both feeling aroused. Natasha keeps moving her hand to my crotch. She gently and discreetly fondles my cock, keeping me hard. It feels amazing. I watch Nissa being very playful and affectionate with Andrea. She touches her often during the conversations. She always agrees with whatever Andrea is saying, sometimes kissing her shoulder or cheek. During desert I notice a familiar crazed look on my sweetheart's face. I'm pretty sure Nissa has her hand up Andrea's dress and is playing with her pussy.

After dinner, everyone says their good-byes. Both the men and ladies all hug and kiss Andrea, Nissa and Natasha. I'm the odd dressed duck who gets the polite handshakes.

We wait near the exit while Nissa chats with Derek and Joseph. Once we're in the elevator Andrea and I profusely thank Nissa.

"You two are very welcome. Andrea my sweet candy, you were so adorable, everyone loves you. And Andrew….I know you felt uncomfortable at times. Cherish how amazing everything was. And you did have my beautiful Natasha by your side."

"I agree, I had an amazing time. On the next cruise I'll bring my tux…. just in case!"

Nissa continues, "so the evening is still young. I'm always full of wonderful surprises. Derek and Joseph have invited us to their penthouse suite. I promise it will be better than you can ever imagine."

Andrea claps her hands together and yells "Yes! Yes!" She quickly turns to me. She throws her arms around me hugging me tightly. As she pulls back, she kisses me passionately, then looking as adorable as possible she asks, "Can we go?"

I cannot tell you how much it meant for my sweetheart to show me that she hadn't forgotten about me. We were still a team exploring this crazy journey together. I kissed her nose. "Of course! This is our last night with our amazing friends. Let's get this party started!"

At the opposite end of the ship are the two other penthouse suites. One door white, the other a deep purple. Joseph opens the purple door. He's wearing a silk robe. The ladies enter first, all getting hugs and kisses. I enter last. I'm trying hard not to feel awkward. I hate my beige dockers and shirt! This time Joseph smiles and grabs my hand. "Come with me!"

He takes me into a luxurious ornate bathroom, where he hands me a silk robe. "Take off those dreadful clothes and put this on." He gives me a hug. "We're sorry if we made you feel weird. I can help you undress.... or not." I don't know what to say. Joseph smiles, "Come join us when you're ready." He leaves. I'm feeling way better. I quickly change and join everyone in the salon.

As I enter, everyone applauds and cheers. I take a short bow. Derek approaches. He gives me a look up and down, then smiles. "Welcome to our party. You look fantastic." He hugs me tight. One of his hands slides down my back and across my ass. As he steps back, he turns to everyone and says, "You are correct Nissa, he is very muscular." Everyone cheers again.

Natasha hands me a glass of......CLIX vodka of course. On ice with a sliver of lemon. For the next thirty minutes or so everyone is immersed in conversation. To my delight, my sweetheart is by my side the entire time. Every so often we have a moment to look around. The floor is the same white marble with gold veins. The walls are covered in erotic tapestries. The sliver of light that surrounds the room changes from white to blue to purple, then pink. Instead of faux furs on the floor, there are thick squares of white and gold plush carpet.

Derek and Joseph are so nice, so friendly. They're both in silk robes, nothing else. Derek is slightly taller than me, maybe six foot one. He has a nice muscular physique. He seems to be the dominate one. Joseph is my height, five foot eleven. Like me, he's leaner. But we're both in excellent shape with a more defined muscular build. His mannerisms are slightly feminine. They live and work in Los Angeles. They own a night club as well as several BDSM leather and fetish stores. Derek is Ukrainian. Joseph is from San Francisco.

Derek clinks his glass to get everyone's attention. "We are all now getting to know each other. Sadly, it is our last night. But…. our last night is not over until we see the sun! Come. Everyone come!" As we all gather around the bar, I see Derek also has a small ornate box. He places it on the table, next to a rectangular mirror. Carefully he lays out and begins chopping a somewhat large pile of white luminescent powder into a fine dust. He than draws out two lines for everyone. I notice that this powder has a slight hint of blue in it. I look at Andrea, who shrugs her shoulders. We're all feeling the affects of champagne, wine, cognac and vodka! The coke we enjoyed at Nissa's has worn off. We all take our turn and snort a line of Derek's magical powder into each nostril. The affect is almost immediate. It's like the most wonderful jolt of adrenaline imaginable. Everyone is energized. The ladies disappear to the bathroom and return in short silk robes. Joseph turns up the music and dims the lights. Soon everyone is dancing. We're all laughing and having a great time. The party is on! Derek and Joseph are the first to toss their robes into the air and dance naked. I'm next. For the first time I can see our naked bodies. All of us look great. All of us have beautiful cocks. The ladies cheer. Andrea of course is the first to toss her robe into the air. Wow! She is so fucking hot. Everyone admires her perfect ass, perfect breasts and smoking hot legs. Nissa tosses her robe next, striking several poses. Her well-defined muscular body blows everyone's mind. She is fucking hot! We all applaud. Natasha moves to the center and slowly peels her robe off her shoulders, letting it fall to her waist. Her skin is a sexy pale white. Natasha's back, shoulders and arms are slender. She has long beautiful legs. She reveals her small tight ass. No doubt, Natasha is one sexy creature. Everyone's eyes are glued to Natasha's robe. Then in a flash she tosses it into the air revealing the most beautiful cock I have ever seen. I don't want to stare, but I have never seen a cock that was so feminine......yet it's a cock. Everyone cheers and the dancing resumes. Everyone's naked.

After a series of songs, the music dims down. Derek claps his hands. All eyes turn to Derek. He takes Joseph's hand. Joseph reaches out and takes Nissa's hand. She takes Andrea's hand, who takes Natasha's, who takes mine. Derek leads us into their bedroom. There are three king size beds in the center of the room pushed together into a triangle of sorts. I can hear the faint sound of mood music. We all surround the beds. Following Dereks lead, we climb onto the beds and begin kissing each other…touching each other. Whatever we have snorted makes me feel so alive. My cock is hard. I can feel it throbbing. I love it. I watch Andrea kiss Nissa, then Derek. Natasha kisses me. I feel someone's hands caressing my back, then my ass. I turn. Joseph kisses me. I feel his hands stroke my cock. This is a first for me…. but I don't care. I'm lost in lust and desire. My hands move down his body. He's smooth yet firm and muscular. Natasha moves closer, the three of us begin kissing and touching each other.

I look across the bed for Andrea. She's on her back with her legs spread. Nissa is on all fours eating Andrea's pussy. Derek is fucking Nissa from behind.

Natasha turns, facing both Joseph and me. She presses her hands on our chests and slowly drifts down passed our flat stomachs to our hard cocks. She strokes both of us. She drops to her knees and begins sucking our cocks, back and forth. It feels amazing. Natasha looks amazing. She rises, she kisses me passionately pressing her tongue into my mouth. She pulls back so that we are eye to eye. "Suck me."

Yes, I'm high on some incredible drug. Yes, I'm immersed in this wonderful sexual trance. And no, I don't want to disrupt this incredible sexual orgy by rejecting Natasha.... who's fucking hot. I suck on her nipples, then drop to my knees. Holy fuck! I haven't ever been this close to another cock.... not even my own! Natasha senses this is so strange for me. "Close your eyes baby. Trust me."

WTF. I'm in this crazy sexually aroused state.... everyone is. I close my eyes. I let Natasha press her cock into my mouth. It feels so strange. Her cock is slender and hard. I can't describe the sensations in my mouth or my mind. My tongue feels all her nuances. I hear her moans of pleasure. My cock throbs. I let all my worries go. I'm immersed in this new experience. Slowly Natasha presses her cock deeper, then she slowly withdraws. Each time her pace increases. Each time she moans with pleasure. "You feel so good baby." Soon she's fucking my mouth. I feel her hands grasp my head. She increases her pace. She moans loudly. Is she going to cum? Suddenly, she withdraws. She then presses her cock back into my mouth…. but I immediately realize this is not Natasha! This cock is thicker, bigger…. I immediately open my eyes, its Joseph. Natasha kneels next to me. She places her hand on my shoulder. "Go with it, Andrew. We're all sensual creatures." I don't resist. I allow Joseph to continue. In and out he slowly fucks my mouth. His moans of pleasure remind me of myself. After a few minutes, Joseph withdraws. I feel Natasha pull me up. She kisses me hard. "You are amazing. Fuck me." She bends over showing me her sexy hot ass. She pulls her cheeks apart exposing her ass button. I move in closer. I'm no doubt immersed in the craziest experience of my life. I press my throbbing cock up into Natasha's ass. The sensation is tight, snug and wet. I press deeper. Natasha moans loudly. "Yes baby. Deeper." Soon my cock is fully up her ass. My cock throbs. Slowly I begin fucking her.

I glance around the beds. Where's my sweetheart? Is she watching me? Did she see me sucking a cock? There she is……on all fours. Joseph is now fucking my baby….and Derek's fucking her mouth! We indeed have become nymphos!

Watching her arouses me more. I amp up my fucking of Natasha's ass.

I feel a hand on my back. It's Nissa. "Good boy Andrew. Fuck her hard."

Natasha agrees, "Fuck me! Fuck my ass!"

I become a crazy person. I begin pounding Natasha deep and hard. Bam! Bam! Bam! I can't stop. I'm possessed.

Nissa loves it. "Yes! Go Andrew! Fuck her ass!"

Natasha is caught up in the moment as well. "Harder! Harder!"

My urge to cum builds, stronger and stronger. I try to hold back, but I can't. I let out a primordial yell as I explode into Natasha's ass. It feels fantastic. At the same time, I hear Joseph cum, and then Derek. I withdraw. I drop to my knees. I'm spent. Slowly I crawl towards my sweetheart who is lying quietly alone. I cuddle up behind her, kissing her back, then her neck. She smiles. "Thank you for finding me. I need you. I feel safe now."

Derek and Joseph quietly lay together as does Nissa and Natasha. The orgy has subsided. The magical drug has left us exhausted. We quietly fall asleep.

Day 8   Bon Voyage

It's probably around eight in the morning when Joseph wakes us. "Wake up sleepy heads. I'm sorry to disturb you. But we all must be off the ship in a few hours. I'm sure you need to pack."

Whoa! That's an eye opener! We quickly sit up. Nissa and Natasha have already left. We put on our robes and get up to find our clothes. In the salon Derek greets us. "Good morning. There's coffee and orange juice on the bar. No rush, you have four hours."

Andrea and I dress. We quickly down a glass of orange juice. Andrea hugs and kisses both Derek and Joseph. They both hug me. I feel Joseph kiss my neck. We say our good-byes and thank them for an amazing experience.

Back in our rooms we shower and begin packing. Andrea looks over at me and says, "Do you want to talk about last night?"

I respond, "Do you?"

There's no hesitation from Andrea. "Absolutely yes! A thousand times yes!"

Oh fuck. What did she see? "I guess that means, you're sure."

"Andrew! Ten thousand times yes!"

"Okay. Let's finish packing....and you're going first!"

Andrea laughs. "Andrew you're so forceful."

We finish our packing with an hour to spare. We hurry to the promenade hoping to find something to eat. We're starving! Fortunately, we're able to still get coffee and two bagels.

We find an isolated table. Once seated, Andrea is anxious to get started. "Okay, I'll go first."

She pauses for a moment then blurts out, "Holy fuck! Was that crazy or what!   I can't believe it even happened."

Andrea stands up. She clasps her hands together. "Holy fuck! They're all nymphos! What was that shit we put up noses? It sure the hell was more than just coke."

Andrea sits back down.

"Okay baby, calm down. I agree last night was crazy. For sure the coke was laced with something. I remember it looked blue. Are you feeling okay?"

Andrea seems to be calmer now that she has vented. "I'm fine. But fuck. What a finale. Dinner was amazing. I was feeling so happy...and turned on. I can't believe Nissa had her finger in my pussy at the dinner table! Do you think anyone saw?"

"I don't know. I knew something was going on. You had that crazed look on your face. All four of us were high. How do you feel about what happened in the penthouse?"

Andrea's eyes widened. "Whatever that blue powder was, it was fucking amazing. It lit me up. I felt great. Everything was great. The music rocked. Dancing naked was soooo fun!"

Well, it appears my sweetheart enjoyed our crazy orgy. "Keep going."

Andrea continues, "It turned me on when we all held hands and walked into their bedroom. Circling the beds was like a cult ritual. The bed was our alter. Then everyone climbed onto the bed and started kissing and touching. I felt my nipples getting hard. Nissa started playing with my pussy. I was so wet. Then Derek joined us. He smelled amazing. He's so muscular. He was kissing and touching us both. They're both Doms. Nissa commanded me to eat her pussy. Derek commanded me to suck his cock. It was a trip! I was like a sex slave."

Andrea pauses. "I'm sorry, I'm carrying on. Should I stop? I don't need to get into all the details. I'll just say it was a crazy experience."

I must admit there is a part of me that gets turned on hearing the details. And there's a part of me not so sure how I feel. But when I think about what I was immersed in....and totally enjoying it, I have to appreciate Andrea's excitement.

"No, I love that we're exploring our sexual fantasies together. Whatever that sex drug was, it intensified everything."

I can tell Andrea wants to share more. "Yes! Everything was intense.... in a good way. I remember Nissa crawling away towards you, and suddenly Joseph joined in with Derek. They both took turns fucking me. My pussy was so wet."

Andrea leans in and lowers her voice. "Andrew, they were fucking my mouth. It was a strange sensation. I felt like I was in a porn movie."

Andrea sits back up. She doesn't say if she liked it or not....and I'm not asking. For me that was TMI. My sweetheart is indeed a nympho.

Andrea is all perky. "Okay, your turn!"

Fuck. Where do I start? Do I really want to share my bi-sexual experience? This is a hard one for me. Am I ashamed? Do I act excited about having Natasha and Joseph's cocks in my mouth?

Andrea sees my hesitation. "Andrew are you okay? No matter what happened, if you enjoyed yourself, I'm excited to hear about it."

I'm frozen. Where do I begin. Andrea tries to help. "You were with Natasha and Joseph. All three of you have cocks. That's a first for you. I'm pretty sure Natasha was into sucking you. Joseph's gay. Did he suck you too?"

My response is, "yes, yes and yes."

Andreas confused, but only for a second. "Yes, Natasha sucked your cock. Yes, Joseph sucked your cock. And.... yes?......you sucked them!"

"It wasn't my idea! And I didn't want to spoil the mood. It just kind of happened."

Andrea leans over and hugs me. "Andrew! That is so cool. Did you like it? Natasha's cock isn't that big…. but Joseph's is like yours!"

Mentally I thank my sweetheart for being so excited and interested in my experience. I feel my hesitation and fear fall away. For the first time in my life, I feel totally liberated. My fears of being judged are replaced with the excitement of sharing my experience. Wow! I love my nympho!

"I'm not sure I can say I loved it. It was so unexpected and different. I was also worried what you might think if you saw what was happening. I should have been more like you…. just immersed in the experience. You love being a nympho. I need to embrace every experience and not worry. Like you said, we were all nymphos!"

We talked more about my experience. I shared in detail what it was like to fuck Natasha up her ass. I shared my fear when I thought Natasha was going to cum in my mouth. All in all, it was a wonderful moment of non-judgmental openness.

Our week on a Sex Cruise was indeed life changing for both of us. We discovered our love for sex. Each experience brought us closer as a couple. We are more in love than ever before. We're both excited to be in the lifestyle. We can't wait to visit

Nissa and Natasha in New York. And who knows, maybe we'll go visit Derek and Joseph?

Thank you so much for reading my fun erotic story. Although this crazy story is mostly a figment of my vivid imagination, a lot of my story came from a real cruise I bravely took in 2021. This is my second book. Please consider reading my first book, The Obsession. It's a story about a young man who becomes consumed with lust and love for a young girl who lives across the lake.

I'm fortunate to reside in a small town in northern California, where art and wine rule. Please check out my websites, www.StevieGreenfield.com or www.etsy.com/shop/StevieEroticArt

www.ingramcontent.com/pod-product-compliance
Lightning Source LLC
Chambersburg PA
CBHW070344130626
46556CB00007B/3031